W9-BPM-099

THE SEARCH FOR
SIDNEY'S SMILE

THE SEARCH FOR SIDNEY'S SMILE

BY MARC KORNBLATT

ILLUSTRATED BY
JOHN STEVEN GURNEY

SIMON & SCHUSTER BOOKS FOR YOUNG READERS
Published by Simon & Schuster
New York • London • Toronto • Sydney • Tokyo • Singapore

Sidney woke up from his nap feeling sad.
  "What's the matter, Sidney?" asked Daddy.
"Did you lose your smile somewhere?"
  Sidney answered with a frown.
"Come on," said Daddy. "Let's go find it."

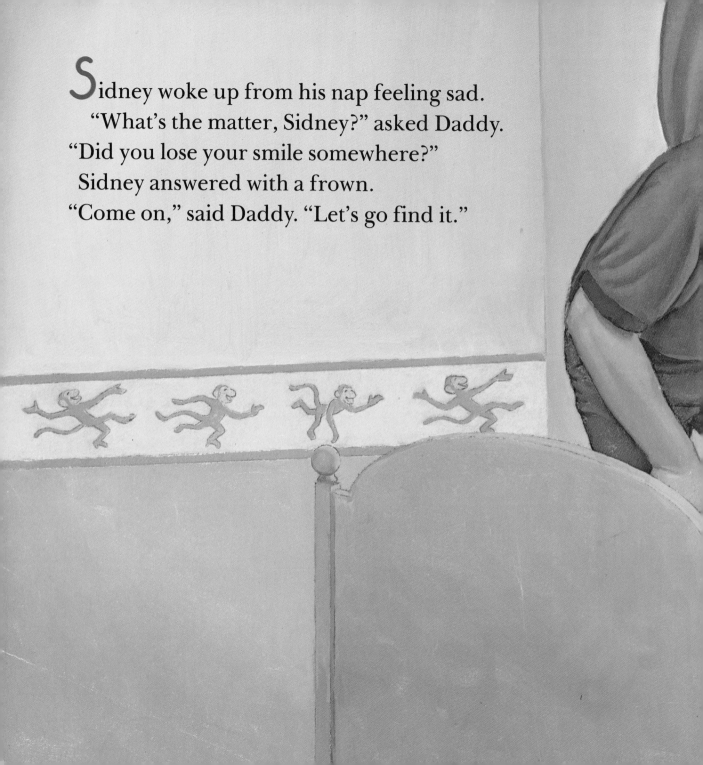

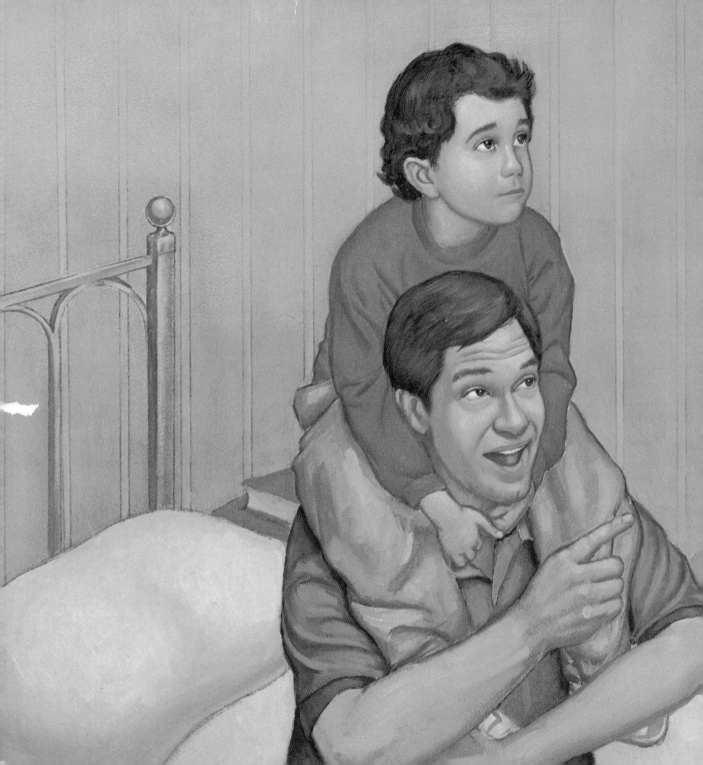

First, they searched in Daddy's bedroom.
"Do you see it on the ceiling?"
No, it wasn't there.
Next, they tried the kitchen.

"Could your smile be in this carton?"
Not there, either.
Then they went down to the basement.

"Did you leave it on the moon, Sidney?"
No, not on the moon.
They visited the playground.

"Maybe it's hiding in here."
No.
Next, they went to the zoo.

"Did the monkey steal your smile,
Sidney?" No, he didn't.
They even looked inside a
movie theater.

CHIMPANZEE

"It's not here?"
Nope.
After that, they went
back home and Sidney
took a bath.

"Maybe it washed off in the tub."

No. Not there, either.

By then, Daddy was tired. "I give up," he said.
"I can't find your smile anywhere."
Sidney lifted his arms. "Daddy, hold me," he said.

Daddy picked him up and hugged him. Sidney smiled.
  "I should have known," said Daddy. "Your smile just
got stuck inside.
All you needed was a good squeeze to push it out."
When he hugged him again, Sidney laughed.

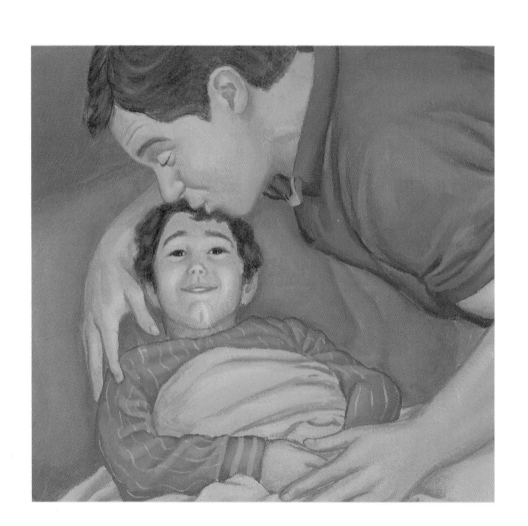

For Jacob
—MK

With love to Kathie and special thanks
to Phillip and Michael
—JSG

SIMON & SCHUSTER BOOKS FOR YOUNG READERS
Simon & Schuster Building, Rockefeller Center
1230 Avenue of the Americas, New York, New York 10020
Text copyright © 1993 by Marc Kornblatt
Illustrations copyright © 1993 by John Gurney
All rights reserved including the right of reproduction
in whole or in part in any form.
SIMON & SCHUSTER BOOKS FOR YOUNG READERS
is a trademark of Simon & Schuster.
Designed by Vicki Kalajian.
The text for this book was set in 17 pt. Baskerville.
The illustrations are reproduced from oil paintings.
Also available in a LITTLE SIMON paperback edition.
Manufactured in the United States of America
10 9 8 7 6 5 4 3 2 1

Library of Congress Cataloging-in-Publication Data
Kornblatt, Marc. Search for Sidney's smile / by Marc Kornblatt ;
illustrated by John Gurney.   p. cm.   Summary: When Sidney wakes up from his nap,
his smile is gone, and he and his father spend the rest of the day
looking everywhere for it.
[1. Fathers and sons—Fiction.   2. Smile—Fiction.]   I. Gurney, John, ill.   II. Title.
PZ7.K8373Se   1993   [E]—dc20   92-12824   CIP
ISBN: 0-671-76912-X   ISBN: 0-671-76913-8 (pbk)